I'm a Great Big
EIGHTEEN-WHEELER!

by Michael Anthony Steele
Illustrated by Richard Courtney and Tom LaPadula

SCHOLASTIC INC.

New York   Toronto   London   Auckland   Sydney

Mexico City   New Delhi   Hong Kong   Buenos Aires

HASBRO and its logo, and TONKA are trademarks of Hasbro and are used with permission. ©2003 Hasbro. All Rights Reserved.

Published by Scholastic Inc.
SCHOLASTIC and associated logos are trademarks and/or registered trademarks of Scholastic Inc.

Library of Congress Cataloging-in-Publication Data Available

ISBN 0-439-48724-2

10 9 8 7 6 5 4 3 2 1   03 04 05 06 07
Designed by Carisa Swenson

Printed in the U.S.A.
First printing, August 2003

I'm a great big eighteen-wheeler!

I haul great big loads . . .

. . . so I need eighteen great big wheels!

Once I hauled a trailer full of cars.

Another time, I hauled a trailer full of cows.

And once I pulled a great big house down the road!

Now I'm hauling a great big trailer of food to a grocery store.

I have great big mirrors!
They let my driver see other cars.

Sometimes I get weighed on a great big scale.

It checks to see that I'm not too heavy.

Uh-oh! It's getting late.

I'd better pull into a truck stop to spend the night.

My driver sleeps in a special part of the cab called a sleeper.

My sleeper has a bed, a TV, a refrigerator, and even a microwave oven!

As soon as my trailer is empty, I'll go on a new job!

Now I get to haul a heavy load of bricks!